PRINCESS TALES

ONCE UPON A TIME IN RHYME WITH SEEK-AND-FIND PICTURES

ADAPTED BY
GRACE MACCARONE

ILLUSTRATED BY
GAIL DE MARCKEN

FEIWEL AND FRIENDS

NEW YORK

SEEK AND FIND

EXPLORE THE WORLD OF ONCE UPON A TIME.

Read the stories. Then pore over pictures filled with treasures and trinkets. And join the quest to find hidden objects in the list that accompanies each illustration. After you're done, explore some more. You may find references to your favorite poems and rhymes. In every picture, look for the boy below, the fluffy dog, the white cat, the checked pattern, the red scarf, the baseball cap, and one or more golden doves. Good luck!

Table of Contents

CINDERELLA

As Cinderella worked all day,
she had no time to dream or play.
"Dust the shelves!" her stepmom said.
"Fold the laundry! Make my bed!
Wash the windows! Scrub the floor!
When you're done, I'll find you more!"
Her haughty daughters had no pity.
They were proud and weren't pretty,
but Cinderella tried her best
to do her work and please the rest.
One day, a fairy came to call
and said, "You're going to a ball.
I'll change six lizards into men,
six mice will be six horses, then
this pumpkin coach will take you there,
and here's a dress for you to wear.
But, Cinderella, be aware,
at twelve o'clock, my spell will end,
so leave before that, my sweet friend."
With Cinderella at the dance,
no other maiden had a chance.
The prince and Cinderella talked
and laughed and ate and danced and walked.
She ran away when midnight came,
never having said her name.
In disbelief, the prince ran, too.
He lost the girl, but found a shoe.
"At least," he said, "I have a clue,
a shoe that fits my future bride."
He searched his kingdom, far and wide.
The sisters tried it, then their mother.
The prince inquired, "Is there no other?"
Then Cinderella burst, "It's mine!"
She slipped it on, and it fit fine.
"Be mine," said he. "Oh, yes," she said.
The happy couple now is wed.

Find 3 fiddlers, a flag, 2 watches, a wand, and a see-through shoe.

THUMBELINA

From a seed of barleycorn,
Thumbelina would be born.
The seed was planted. Then in two
months' time, a yellow flower grew.
The flower petals opened wide.
They held the tiny girl inside.
Though very pretty, she was slight,
and only half a thumb in height.
A mother toad hopped by one night,
delighted by the lovely sight
of Thumbelina in her bed,

a nutshell. Then the mother said,
"I'll take this pretty little one
to be the bride of my dear son."
And Thumbelina later woke
to nasty sounds: the toad son's croak!
Stranded on a lily leaf,
the homesick girl was filled with grief.
With water on her every side,
the frightened girl was trapped. She cried,
"Don't make me be that toad son's bride."
Luckily, a school of fish
heard her cries and heard her wish.
They bit the stem so she could float

upriver in her lily boat.
Seeing her from up above,
a flying beetle fell in love,
took Thumbelina to his tree,
and all his friends came out to see.
"But she's so ugly," said his friends.
The beetle took her down again.
Eating nectar, drinking dew,
all alone, all summer through
to winter, when the cold winds blew
and food was scarce, the small one knew
she needed help. What *would* she do?
She found a little wooden door

that led beneath the forest floor.
The door was opened by a mouse
who let the girl inside her house.
Mouse's friend was Mr. Mole;
he'd often visit Mouse's hole.
He liked the dark, for he was blind.
Though he was rich, he was not kind.
Nearby, a bird lay frozen dead.
The mole would kick him in the head.
One night, the small girl left her bed.
She made a blanket. Then she spread
it on the bird who woke again.
The sickly bird said, "Thank you. When

I'm well and strong, I'll fly away.
But now I'm weak, so I will stay."
The kind girl nursed him every day.
Then by-and-by, the old mole tried
to make the gentle girl his bride.
"Marry him," said Mrs. Mouse,
"and you will have a lovely house."
The helpless girl was horrified.
But meanwhile, Thumbelina tried
her best to heal the ailing bird.
When he was well, he kept his word.
As he was able, off he flew—
the bird and Thumbelina, too—

above the shores, above the seas,
above the hills, above the trees.
They landed in a poppy bed.
"I'll settle here," the small girl said.
Surprised, she saw a tiny king
who offered her a tiny ring.
"Please be my wife," the wee king said.
He put his crown upon her head.
Then many teeny folk appeared.
They saw their king and queen, and cheered!

Find 3 umbrellas, a nutshell, 4 red shoes, a ladybug,
7 beetles, a fly, 4 fish eyes, and 2 dragonflies.

Beauty and the Beast

In a faraway land, this story goes,
a widowed father plucked a rose,
belonging to a Beast, who would
have killed the man right where he stood.
The man asked, "May I say good-bye
to my dear child before I die?"
The Beast said, "I will set you free
if she agrees to live with me."
As fair of face as she was good,
the girl, called Beauty, said she would.
Beauty did not hesitate
and soon, she reached the palace gate.
Such opulence she'd never seen!
The girl was treated like a queen.
At suppertime a splendid feast
appeared, like magic, then the Beast,
so awful, Beauty could not bear
his monstrous face, yet she would stare
into his soulful, searching eyes,
revealing something kind and wise.
Beauty tried to hide her fear.
Beast asked, "Could you be happy here?"
As Beast and Beauty passed an hour,
a friendship soon began to flower.
"Can you love me?" poor Beast sighed.
"I cannot," the girl replied.

That night, a prince in Beauty's dream,
said, "Things are not as they might seem.
Trust what you feel, not what you see.
Your gratitude will set me free."
With pleasant ways to pass the hours—
ribbons and silks for making flowers,
gardens to walk, instruments to play,
magical birds that talked all day,
paintings to ponder, books to read—
the Beast met Beauty's every need.
As Beast and Beauty better knew
each other, so their fondness grew.
The poor Beast begged, "Please, be my bride."
"I cannot," the girl replied.
At night, the prince in Beauty's dream,
said, "Things are not as they might seem.
Trust what you feel, not what you see.
Your gratitude will set me free."
Now many happy months had past,
the girl and Beast were friends at last.
One day, Beast saw the Beauty cry,
and through her sobs, she told him why.
"I long to see my home once more
and see the father I adore."

Find an arrow, a horn, a gold rat, and a grey mouse.

The Beast said, "I will let you go,
but there is something you should know.
You must return, for if you lie
and two months pass, then I will die."
The girl became ecstatic when
she saw her father's face again.
So Beauty, now of some renown,
upon returning to her town,
was welcomed back by one and all.
Her friends and neighbors came to call.
And so two months went quickly by;
her time at home had seemed to fly.
So busy, Beauty didn't know
the time had come for her to go,
not thinking of her dearest friend,
whose life was coming to an end.
That night, she dreamed the Beast was lying
near a cave and slowly dying.
She rushed to him without delaying,
crying as she ran, and praying.
If she could only save his life,
she would agree to be his wife.
She found the Beast upon his bed.
He lay so still, she thought him dead.
She sprinkled water on his head;
she hoped the water would revive
him, and it did. Beast was alive!
"I love you, Beast," the Beauty said.
Now not a Beast, a prince instead.
And Beauty and the prince were wed.
Beauty's love reversed a spell.
Love conquers all; now all is well.

Find 2 loaves, a paintbrush, a parrot, and a yellow bouquet.

SNOW WHITE

A queen had a daughter, long ago,
with red-rose lips, skin white as snow,
with sea-blue eyes, hair black as night;
the parents named the child Snow White.
Misfortune struck; the good queen died.
The king, obliged to take a bride,
then wed a woman, full of pride.
With each new day, she rose from bed,
approached her glass, and vainly said,

"Magic mirror, in my hand,
who is fairest in the land?"

The queen would not be satisfied
until the looking glass replied,

"Oh, lovely queen, I tell you true:
The fairest in the land is you."

But as time passed, fair Snow White grew
in character and beauty, too.
And then one day, the queen would hear
the mirror state her greatest fear:

"There is a girl, sublime and bright.
Surpassing all, she is Snow White."

Her nostrils smoked, her eyes burned red,

the queen proclaimed, "I want her dead!"
Her huntsman tried, but could not slay
Snow White. He said, "Run far away!"
He left her in the deep, dark wood.
She gathered all the strength she could.
Afraid, she ran and ran some more,
collapsing on the forest floor.
"I'm all alone," poor Snow White feared.
The girl was wrong; a house appeared.
With hope that she could rest inside,
she pressed the door; it opened wide.
The room was small, but clean and neat,
with one long table, seven seats,
and seven little loaves of bread

on seven plates, and seven beds.
But finding that she couldn't keep
awake, the princess fell asleep.
And when she was alert again,
about her, seven tiny men,
delighted by this lovely sight,
invited her to stay the night.
The princess told her tale of woe;
they said she needn't ever go
if she would clean and cook and sew.
Aware the forest held great dangers,
they said to her, "Beware of strangers!"
At dawn, the queen arose from bed.
She held her mirror, then she said,

"Magic mirror, in my hand,
who is fairest in the land?"

The mirror spoke: "I tell you true.
Snow White is far more fair than you.
The cottage where the good dwarves dwell—
Snow White is there, alive and well."

Enraged and shocked, the vain queen said,
"I cannot rest until she's dead!"
The seven dwarves went off to work;
outside the cottage, evil lurked.
Through the forest came a hag,
a poison apple in her bag.
Snow White didn't realize

the evil queen was in disguise.
Over-trusting, poor Snow White
allowed herself to take a bite.
The lovely princess quickly died;
the wicked queen was satisfied.
The seven dwarves were horrified.
They built her coffin, teary-eyed.
A noble prince, out for a ride
upon his stallion, somehow spied
the coffin with Snow White inside.
He kissed her, and she came to life.
The prince asked her to be his wife.

*Find a pig in a hurry, a spider and a fly, 2 webs,
2 squirrels, 3 butterflies, and 3 bears.*

13

The Princess and the Frog

Long ago, an emperor's daughter
lost her ball in deepest water.
Distraught, the princess cried and cried,
and soon a frog was by her side.
Responding to her caterwaul,
he learned the princess lost her ball.
"What can I have? What will you do
if I can get your ball for you?"
he asked. She answered, "Golden crowns
and ruby rings and silken gowns."
"Not crowns, not gowns," the bullfrog said.
"I want to be your friend instead,
to play with you, to share your bread,
to read with you, to share your bed."
She didn't want to, nonetheless,
to have her ball, she told him, "Yes,
I'll do exactly as you say."
He got her ball. She ran away.
"Wait for me!" the poor frog said.
By then, the girl was far ahead.
The princess dined at six o'clock,
and at that time, she heard a knock.
Rushing up to get the door,
she found the frog upon the floor.
The frog said, "Let me enter," but
she pushed the door and slammed it shut.
Returning quickly to her seat,
the princess was too shocked to eat.
"Why do you tremble?" asked the king.
The princess told him everything.

Find a broom, 2 pandas, an elephant, and a dragon in a tree.

He said, "A promise must be kept."
The princess shook her head and wept.
"I shall obey," the girl replied.
The princess let the frog inside.
The frog said, "Put me in your chair."
The princess didn't want him there.
The king remarked when she delayed;
the princess dutifully obeyed.
The frog said, "Let me share your plate."
The princess couldn't tolerate
the pushy frog; alas! The king
would have her sharing everything!
The frog ate blithely while he croaked;
while, as she ate, the princess choked.
"I'm tired now," the bold frog said.
"Tonight, I'll get to share your bed."
The princess picked him up with care
and took him quickly up the stair.
It was, however, plain to see
she didn't do it willingly.
And when the princess reached her room,
an impish smile began to bloom.
She wouldn't put him on her bed;
she threw him at the wall instead.
Amazingly, a magic spell
was broken as the bullfrog fell.
The frog was changed, and in its place:
a prince with kindly eyes and face.
Returning to his human life,
he asked the girl to be his wife.
She told the prince, "I'll cherish you
for all my days," and it was true.

Find a kettle, 2 monkeys, 2 dragons, and a rabbit. Then
follow frog prints to the frog and mud drops to the prince.

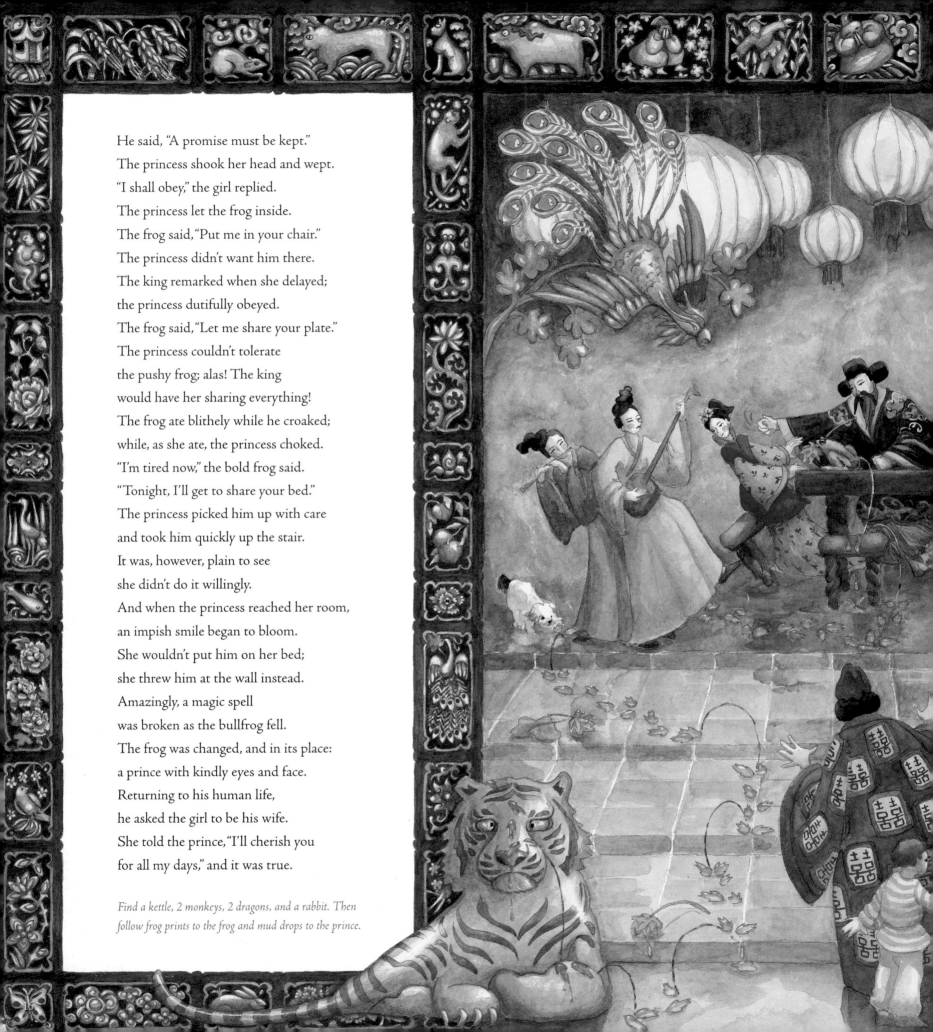

THE PRINCESS AND THE PEA

A prince had travelled far and wide
to seek a princess as his bride.
To spot a princess who was true
was not an easy thing to do.
"I give up," the poor prince cried.
He went back home without a bride.
One evening, cold winds blew; it poured
and lightning flashed and thunder roared.
Alas! Although the hour was late,
a girl was at the castle gate.
The girl was quite a ghastly sight
from travelling on that stormy night,
with dripping hair and rain-drenched clothes
and soggy shoes and sopping hose.
She claimed to be a princess, though,
if it were true, it didn't show.
The prince inquired, "How can we know?"
"I have a plan," his mother said.
"I'll put a pea beneath her bed.
And twenty cushions on the pea.
In the morning, we shall see."
The princess, on the pea all night,
by daybreak, was an awful sight.
"I couldn't sleep. I'm black and blue,"
the princess said, for she was true.
A girl so sensitive to feel
a pea was absolutely real.
The prince was grateful all his life
to have this princess as his wife.

Find 4 snakes, 2 giraffes, 2 red birds, a black hen, and a pea.

RUMPELSTILTSKIN

A miller, meeting with a king,
told the king an untrue thing:
"My daughter changes straw to gold."
The king replied, "I must behold
this wondrous feat. Please, bring her here."
The miller's daughter, full of fear,
arrived at once. The room she saw
was floor-to-ceiling filled with straw.
"As a test," the king then told
her, "Here is straw to spin to gold.
If you cannot, then you will die."
The frightened girl could not reply.

He shut the door and locked her in
and left the girl all night to spin.
Alone, the miller's daughter cried;
she wondered why her father lied.
Just then, a tiny man appeared.
He said, "What's wrong?" She said she feared
that she would surely die unless
she spun pure gold from this straw mess.
He said, "That's something I can do,
but I must have a gift from you."
"Take my ring," the daughter pled.
"Your ring will do," the strange man said.
He turned the wheel; all night he spun.
By daybreak, all the work was done.

The king was pleased, but wanted more.
He filled a room with straw from floor
to ceiling, but he stopped before
he turned the key to lock the door.
The king beheld the girl and said,
"If you finish, we'll be wed.
If you fail, then you'll be dead."
He locked the door and went to bed.
"I'm doomed," the miller's daughter feared.
And once again, the man appeared.
"This is something I can do,
but I must have a gift from you."
"But I have nothing left for you,"
she said. The man said, "Yes, you do."

"I want your firstborn son," he said.
The miller's daughter, filled with dread,
had only this or death to choose.
Either way, the girl would lose.
She said, "You'll get my firstborn boy."
The horrid man was filled with joy.
He turned the wheel; all night he spun.
By daybreak, all the work was done.
The seasons changed; one year had passed.
The princess had a son at last.
The happy mother quite forgot
her bargain, but the man did not.
"I want your child," the small man said.
The princess answered, filled with dread,

"I'll give you treasure. Let him be."
"No treasure is worth more than he.
I'll have the boy," the man replied.
The princess pulled her hair and cried.
He pitied her. "You have three days
to guess my name. You do; he stays."
Although she guessed ten thousand names,
the man's reaction was the same
the first day and the second, too;
the princess didn't have a clue.
Then walking all alone that night,
she came upon a wondrous sight.
Beneath the glowing crescent moon,
the small man danced and sang this tune:

Tomorrow I brew, today I bake,
and then the child away I'll take.
For little deems my royal dame
that Rumpelstiltskin is my name.

The princess, when the morning came,
said, "Rumpelstiltskin is your name."
He stomped his foot, which broke right through
the floor, then tore himself in two.
The princess got to keep her boy,
and all her days were filled with joy.

Find a sun, a moon, 8 cats, a pig, and 6 little mice.

EAST OF THE SUN, WEST OF THE MOON

A family, poor and in despair,
had come to meet a great white bear
who promised he would make them rich.
Predictably, there was a hitch.
"I want a daughter," said the bear,
"the one most honest, kind, and fair."
The youngest daughter said she would
escort the bear, for she was good.
She climbed his back without delay;
the girl and bear were on their way.
Arriving at a mountainside,
a magic portal opened wide
upon a castle, rich and grand,
the finest castle in the land,
so filled with jewels and boundless treasure,
the girl would have her every pleasure:
golden bracelets, diamond crowns,
velvet coats and satin gowns.
The bear said, "What you want is yours,
but stay within your bedroom doors
once evening comes. And never light
a candle in the dark of night.
Having *things* she wanted only,
but no friends, the girl was lonely.
At night, she heard a human crying;
she grabbed a candle, and defying
certain warnings of the bear's,
she ran through doors and down the stairs.
She saw a prince asleep; she stopped.
She was in love. She bent and dropped
some candle wax upon his shirt.

Find 2 bears, 2 reindeer, and four-and-twenty blackbirds.

He blinked his eyes and grew alert.
"By night a man, a bear by day,
I would be free if you obeyed,"
the prince explained. "I have been cursed.
But there is more, and this is worse:
Now you've seen me, I must wed
the long-nosed princess. Woe!" he said.
The prince departed all too soon
for east of the sun, west of the moon.
The girl, in love and in despair,
pursued the prince who'd been a bear.
She passed three women, wise and old,
who gave her curious gifts of gold:
a carding comb, a spinning wheel,
an apple; later, they'd reveal
their use. The women lent a horse
to take the girl along a course
to Brothers Wind—first East, then West
then North and South. She couldn't rest.
Tenaciously, the girl would soon
be east of the sun, and west of the moon.
Once outside the castle wall,
she tossed the apple like a ball.
The long-nosed princess came that way:
"I'd like that apple, if I may.
Please, tell me what I need to pay."
"No money," said the girl, "but might
I get to see the prince tonight?"
The princess said, "Indeed, you can,"
although she had a sneaky plan.
That night, the prince was in his bed,
so sound asleep that he seemed dead.
The desperate girl had tried and tried
to wake the prince, but failed. She cried.
At dawn, outside the royal home,
the girl revealed her carding comb.
Again, the princess came that way
and asked what she would need to pay.

"No money," said the girl, "but might
I get to see the prince tonight?"
The princess said, "Indeed, you can,"
but she'd repeat her sneaky plan.
The girl, no matter what she tried,
would fail to wake the prince. She cried.
At dawn, the princess made a deal
to get the golden spinning wheel.
"I'll let you see the prince," she said,
"tonight. You'll find him in his bed."
But as the prince arose from bed,
a stranger went to him and said,
"Last night, while you were fast asleep,
I could hear a woman weep."
The prince guessed what had come to pass,
so when the princess gave a glass
of mead to him to drink that day,
the wise prince tossed the mead away.
Returning to his room that night,
the girl would find a happy sight—
the prince was wide awake to hatch
a plan to stop his dreadful match.
The prince announced, "My bride-to-be
must clean my favorite shirt for me.
Only a girl with conscience clear
can make this wax spot disappear."
A troll could not; a human could—
a human girl whose heart was good.
The princess tried to clean the spot
of waxy drops, but she could not.
She scrubbed and scrubbed; the stain grew worse.
She was a troll, and she was cursed;
so mad was she, the princess burst.
She left the girl and prince to wed,
contented all their days ahead.

Find a butterfly, 3 bears, and 3 men in a tub.

TWELVE DANCING PRINCESSES

A shepherd, sleeping by a stream,
had met a lady in his dream.
"Go quickly to Beloeil," she said.
"You'll meet a princess whom you'll wed."
The shepherd left without delay.
He reached Beloeil in just one day.
Twelve princesses resided there.
All were proud and all were fair.
The girls were such a lovely sight;
their father locked their room each night
to keep them safe, but every morn,

their pretty shoes were scuffed and torn.
The king was baffled. "How," he said,
"can shoes wear out with feet in bed?"
The princesses would not say why.
"We were asleep," was their reply.
The king announced a proclamation
to every prince in every nation.
"Just tell me where they wear their shoes,"
the king proclaimed, "and you may choose
the one you love to be your bride."
No prince succeeded; many tried.

Arriving at the castle gate,
the shepherd, following his fate,
found employment right away,
making every royal bouquet;
each princess had one—fresh each day.
Eleven did not pay him mind,
but Lina thought his eyes were kind.
The princess liked him, and he knew;
the shepherd liked the princess, too.
At night, the shepherd, in his bed,
was dreaming that the lady said,
"Plant two trees; that's what to do.
Then make a wish. It will come true."
He did as told, and as they grew,

he thought and thought, and then he knew.
Said he, "Invisibility!
For if the daughters can't see me,
I'll follow them the whole night through,
and I'll discover what they do."
One evening, when the girls withdrew
up to their room, the man did, too.
Invisible, but taking space,
he quickly found a hiding place.
The shepherd crawled beneath a bed,
where he remained until one said,
"It's time to go." And climbing out,
he saw such splendor all about—
silken slippers, satin dresses,

jeweled necks, and stylish tresses.
Each princess held the same bouquet
that he had given her that day.
The shepherd thought that they were trapped,
but then the eldest sister clapped,
which opened up a secret door,
and all walked through a corridor,
and down, down, down a winding stair
until they reached a portal where
the princesses and shepherd could
emerge into a pretty wood.
With leaves of silver, gems, and gold,
the trees were dazzling to behold.
Beyond the wood, there was a lake

that held a dozen boats to take
the girls across, and at the oars,
twelve princes rowed to palace shores.
The palace was a splendid sight.
The sisters danced throughout the night.
And that was how the shepherd knew
the secret of the worn-out shoes.
All wondered, *Would the king decide
to let the shepherd choose a bride?*
"I love the shepherd," Lina said.
The king allowed them to be wed.

Find a bridge, 2 bears, 2 squirrels, an elephant's trunk,
a cat, and a fiddle.

SLEEPING BEAUTY

Long ago, a king and queen
begat a child, the fairest seen.
The fairies came to celebrate.
The king, not knowing there were eight,
invited seven. One was slighted.
Angry she was not invited,
in she flew, extremely miffed.
Each fairy gave the child a gift—
she'll sing and dance and move with grace;
have wisdom, wit, a pretty face.
The cross one said, "One day she'll try
a spindle, prick herself, and die!"
The noble king was horrified.
His lady swooned; the fairies cried.
But one last fairy's gift remained.
"She will not die," the last explained.
"Let this gift allay your fears.
The girl will sleep one hundred years.
A noble prince will come, and then
his kiss will wake her up again."
The king then made a proclamation:
"I ban all spindles from the nation."
Near sixteen, the princess, grown,
explored the castle, on her own.

Find 3 balloons, 16 pointe shoes, and 10 princesses.

Inside a room, till then unknown,

an ancient woman lived alone.

Not hearing spindles were forbidden,

she spun her flax, remote and hidden.

The spindle caught the maiden's eye.

"What's this?" she asked. "I'd like to try."

The princess didn't understand

what to do. She cut her hand.

The woman cried, "The princess died!"

The king was quickly at her side.

"Have no fear," the king explained,

"for this event has been ordained.

The princess sleeps; she isn't dead."

Her servants took her to her bed.

Soon, everyone was sleeping, too.

Around the castle, forest grew.

No man or beast could burrow through.

One hundred years had slowly passed.

A noble prince arrived at last.

The prince approached. With every stride,

the thorny thicket opened wide.

All was silent as he crept

within the halls, where dozens slept.

Undaunted by the eerie gloom,

the prince soon found the maiden's room.

He touched her hand; the princess woke.

The spell resolved; the princess spoke:

"I dreamed of you all night and day."

The prince had just one thing to say,

"Then we will marry right away."

They took their vows without delay.

Each child and woman, man and beast

awoke to share the wedding feast.

Find a creamer near a cushion, 2 sleeping squirrels,
and 3 snoozing cranes.

SOURCE NOTES

Mother Goose. Chicago: V.F. Volland, 1915. http://www.gutenberg.org/files/24623/24623-h/24623-h.htm

The Real Mother Goose. Chicago: Rand McNally, 1916. http://www.gutenberg.org/files/10607/10607-h/10607-h.htm#a130

Grimm, Jacob and Wilhelm. *Grimm's Fairy Tales*. Trans. unknown. New York: Puffin Books (London: Penguin Books), 1971 (1823).

Grimm, Jacob and Wilhelm. *Grimm's Fairy Tales* (Household Stories). Trans. Lucy Crane. New York: Book Craft Guild, Inc. (London: Macmillan and Company), 1886.

Grimm, Jacob and Wilhelm. *Grimm's Household Tales*. Trans. Margaret Hunt. London: George Bell and Sons, 1884. http://www.gutenberg.org/cache/epub/5314/pg5314.html

Lang, Andrew. *The Blue Fairy Book*. London: Longman, Green Co. Ltd., 1889. http://www.gutenberg.org/files/503/503-h/503-h.htm#2H_4_0006

Lang, Andrew. *The Yellow Fairy Book*. London: Longman, Green Co. Ltd., 1894.

Perrault, Charles. *The Fairy Tales of Charles Perrault*. Trans. Angela Carter. New York: Avon Books, 1977.

To Jordan Emily, Princess of Popham Hall, who meets her challenges with courage and persistence . . . usually in cargo pants. —G. M.

For Mia and Leo and their friend Hanna. —G. D. M.

A FEIWEL AND FRIENDS BOOK

An Imprint of Macmillan

Feiwel and Friends books may be purchased for business or promotional use. For information on bulk purchases, please contact the Macmillan Corporate and Premium Sales Department at (800) 221-7945 x5442 or by e-mail at specialmarkets@macmillan.com.

Library of Congress Cataloging-in-Publication Data Available
ISBN: 978-0-312-67958-3

The artwork was created with watercolor and ink.

Book design by April Ward

Feiwel and Friends logo designed by Filomena Tuosto

First Edition: 2013

5 7 9 10 8 6 4

mackids.com